Seven for a Secret

http://www.fast-print.net/bookshop

Seven for a Secret

All characters are fictional.
Any similarity to any actual person is purely coincidental.
The right of Sue Evans to be identified as the author of this work has been asserted by her in accordance with the Copyright, Designs, and Patents Act 1988 and any subsequent amendments thereto.

A catalogue record for this book is available from the British Library

ISBN 978-178456-502-2

First published 2018 by
FASTPRINT PUBLISHING
Peterborough, England.

Seven for a Secret

A Novella by
Sue Evans

Printed and bound in England by www.printondemand-worldwide.com

Part 1

Ryan stood at his bedroom window, gazing out into the garden below, deep in thought.

Mother hadn't liked most things, including him, but she had loved the garden in autumn, the russets and browns - her favoured colours.

Alas, she would never look upon it again.

He frowned at the memory of his mother's shocked expression as he stood over her, still gripping the knife dripping with crimson blood. But he felt no sadness.

Now, as he watched the trees swaying in the early morning breeze, a movement caught his eye. It was a magpie settling on a branch, cawing for its mate - it appeared, but wait, another movement higher up in the tree, another two, and on the lawn a pair tending to a younger one.

Seven magpies together a rare sight, befitting a rare day.

A rhyme he had heard came into his mind now.

One for sorrow
Two for joy
Three for a girl, and
Four for a boy
Five for silver
Six for gold, and
Seven for a secret never to be told

His thoughts were interrupted by a gust of wind that scared the magpies into flight. He watched with admiration at their brave struggle against the wind and sympathised with their tireless efforts.

Life could be such a struggle - he knew that more than most.

Ah well, he thought, resigning himself to the fact that they would succeed eventually.

Finally, he was free of his domineering mother; his eyes betrayed a flickering smile.

The smile held a secret, never to be told.

Part 2

The attractive ivy-clad stone building that housed the village art gallery was certainly in-keeping within the picturesque village of Ballacombe. Its white-washed stone cottages huddled amongst the narrow, cobbled streets. It was fit for a picture postcard.

The village nestled at the bottom of a steep-sided ravine looking outwards to the ocean. In the summer, the steep ravine would capture the sun's rays, creating a unique micro climate which attracted scores of tourists.

It was a very different picture in the autumn and winter months when the ravine would trap the harsh winds, thus encouraging the angry waves to thrash up spume against the stone breakwater.

The village was a quiet place at that time of the year. Those locals brave enough to risk the elements would venture to the warmth of the village pub, the Pirate's Rest, owned by a friendly local couple, Fred and Betty Drake. Their collie dog Smithy was a popular and familiar sight on such wintry nights, taking pride of place in front of the pub's open coal fire, ever watchful for tasty titbits coming his way.

The pub was one of the oldest buildings in the village and rumoured to be haunted by the restless spirit of a smuggler known as Tom Gittins. Legend told that in 1756 he was turned over to the authorities by his roguish partner in crime for a reward of ten pieces of silver.

Poor Tom thus met his death at the Gallows Tree, which stood proud near the pub and ancient church. This mighty yew tree was believed to be over one thousand years old.

Allegedly, poor Tom's spirit roamed in torment, forever unable to find peace.

But it was summer now and the village was pregnant with life as Maggie Watts drove into the small car park that graced the front of the art gallery. It was her first day in her newly acquired job as Accounts Manager. From her successful application just three weeks ago it had been a rushed affair.

She now sat in her car, gazing at the front door of the gallery, through which she would shortly enter into her new place of work, her new start in life. She felt a nervous buzz tinged with excitement.

Maggie was thirty-four and presently single, having had her share of live-in lovers and failed relationships. She had become tired of city life and bored with her old job at Abercrombie, Lees & Howell Estate Agents.

In truth, Maggie had reached a crossroads; her life had begun to feel like a jumbled jigsaw with none of the parts fitting together. Something was missing in her life and she desperately needed a change of direction.

In this frame of mind, she had come across the advert for the vacancy at the art gallery, but it was the location that had caught her attention. She had visited Ballacombe as a child whilst holidaying with her parents. These fond childhood memories had always stayed with her, rich and magical, and she had promised herself all those years ago that she would return one day.

That day had arrived.

Part 3

Ryan had been sixteen, the day the magpies came, the day that everything changed in his world.

Until then, he had lived alone with Mother. His father had left for work one day when Ryan was just a small child, and he had never returned. Mother claimed he had abandoned them both so he could take up with his secretary, who she always referred to as 'that blonde tart'.

Ryan had no idea whether this was true or not, his memory of his father having faded long ago. He had been left with only a feeling of betrayal at having been left alone with Mother. Though he could understand why his father had left - in fact, he almost sympathised.

Mother was a monster, with monstrous moods, all of which were bad. Ryan experienced them regularly, his life being a daily dose of misery. School was his only respite, where he was free of violence.

She would yell, throw objects about and display hysterical bouts of screaming, before eventually locking herself away in her room, sometimes for days. During these times, he would attend to his own meals and get himself ready for school.

Sometimes, if the mood was very bad he would hide in the cupboard beneath the stairs. He had placed a pad-lock inside so he could lock himself in and keep the monster out. Sometimes he would be in there for hours until eventually the maelstrom dissipated and he felt secure enough to venture out.

This had been his nightmarish existence until his sixteenth birthday.

Part 4

Ryan liked Betty, the landlady of the Pirate's Rest. She was everything Mother wasn't - caring, loving, always smiling and happy, full of kind words. Fred, her husband, was great too - a father-figure, strong and dependable.

Betty came to the house twice weekly, to clean for Mother. Her visits were the highlights of his week, especially so because she always brought Smithy, their dog, along with her.

Ryan loved Smithy more than anything else in the world. They would play together in the garden for hours, and sometimes Ryan would walk him through the wood at the top of the nearby cliff. This served as a temporary release from the madness of his day-to-day existence.

On cleaning days Ryan would run home from school in anticipation of seeing Smithy; on other days he would dawdle home.

Mother hated Smithy. She would always berate Ryan for touching the filthy old mutt - she always referred to Smithy in those derogatory terms.

Ryan day-dreamed a lot; it was a safe haven in his world where Mother couldn't reach. He dreamed of one day being free to live with Betty, Fred and Smithy, his saviours. Just to lead a normal life like the other children at school - he envied their happiness, an emotion he rarely experienced.

He didn't know his class-mates very well; Mother didn't

encourage his making friends and he had learned the hard way that it was easier to comply with her demands than not.

He never spoke of how Mother treated him - he was too ashamed. He had learned ways to hide his bruises as best he could and would mask his unhappiness by keeping his own company.

He felt so alone sometimes trapped in a nightmare world, his only companion being his growing hatred towards Mother. This fuelled his strength to survive on a day-to-day basis.

He would escape her one day - that was his promise to himself.

That day was fast approaching.

Part 5

Maggie took a deep breath, and climbed out of the car. The day was warm and the sun glinted off the car's bonnet. She felt confident as she made her entrance into the gallery foyer, wearing her most winning smile.

A girl sat behind a desk - she was young, early twenties and very attractive - she beamed up at Maggie with a friendly "Can I help you?"

Maggie smiled "Hi, I'm Maggie, the new girl. Well, 'girl' might be pushing it a bit." She extended her hand in greeting.

The girl stood and accepted her hand. "I'm Eva, so pleased to meet you. The boss, Mr Drake, is away until the weekend but he told me you would be arriving today - I've been instructed to show you the ropes." She rolled her eyes and mimicked a salute.

"Reporting for duty," Maggie replied, returning the salute. She instantly liked Eva; she exuded a natural warmth and friendliness. "What is Mr Drake like? I dealt with an agency throughout the application," she explained.

Eva smirked. "Well he is OK as long as you follow orders and keep your boots shined."

Though the exchange was jovial, Maggie sensed Mr Drake wasn't Eva's best friend. She wondered what he would be like - old, young, pleasant or otherwise.

Eva broke the paused moment "Well, first things first, I

suggest we have some tea and get to know each other, then I'll show you around and we can grab a bite to eat down at the Harbour Bistro at lunch-time"

"Sounds like a good plan," Maggie agreed.

This is a good first day, she thought to herself.

Part 6

Ryan's sixteenth was not to be celebrated of course; Mother did not believe in such things because they involved happiness, enjoyment and good humour - emotions that just simply did not exist in her bitter, twisted world.

He wished he had some friends to invite over but, alas, he had no school friends, and even if he had Mother would have never allowed them to be invited over.

He stared out of the window with only his wishes, but suddenly the sadness evaporated as he spotted Smithy bounding along the lane towards the house, stick in mouth, tail wagging furiously, followed by Betty and Fred.

Realising they had remembered his birthday, his excitement made him race towards the front door so he could be the first to greet them.

Mother intercepted, confronting Betty with a brusque, "Why are you both here? It isn't a cleaning day," her eyes darting between Betty and Fred.

Betty reacted in her usual jovial manner "We've come to wish Ryan a happy birthday, love. I've prepared a surprise birthday lunch for him. Is he about?"

Ryan had reached the front door and ran into Betty's waiting hug. "Thank you so much for calling on my birthday. Can we take Smithy for a walk?"

Betty smiled and nodded in agreement, and Fred grinned,

but Mother didn't smile or grin. She grabbed his arm and berated him. "Control yourself, I will decide if you can go out or not. Do you understand me?" Though this final emphasis was unnecessary, having already made her point clear.

Betty's glance at Fred was a cue. "Well it's not every day a lad is sixteen, I'm sure you won't mind if we steal him for the afternoon," he said calmly but with conviction.

Mother stared at Fred coldly. "Have him home in three hours and in future check with me first." She turned her back, haughtily walking away.

Placing a hand on Ryan's shoulder, Fred ushered him out of the door. "Come on, lad, we'll have you home by 6pm," he assured him.

All thoughts of Mother evaporated the moment Ryan walked away happily with Betty and Fred. Though his last thought that she would be consumed with anger that he was going to celebrate his birthday, despite her protestations, was extremely satisfying.

The stroll back to the Pirate's Rest following the coastal path was fresh and exhilarating.

The meal that Betty had prepared was Ryan's idea of heaven on a plate. She had made all his favourite things, home-made steak pie with hand-cut chips and a mixture of seasonal vegetables grown in Fred's allotment. Dessert was warm apple pie with ice-cream. Ryan insisted that Smithy be given his own portion, which the canine gladly devoured.

The afternoon passed pleasantly, filled with light and easy conversation. Ryan had had the best birthday ever and would always remember it as perfect.

Fred eventually called time, aware that they were under strict orders to get him home by 6pm.

"Well Son, I'd better see you home," Fred said.

Ryan loved to hear Fred call him Son. It made him feel

proud and privileged.

"I've had such a good time, thank you both, and the meal was perfect, Betty," he said truthfully.

"Aw, love, you are most welcome," she replied, hugging him tightly. "It's been a pleasure having you here."

He was sad to leave, but leave he must.

The walk home was cold, and Ryan felt suddenly alone again when Fred left him at the gate. He had had such a nice afternoon, but now he would have to face Mother.

This would be for the last time.

Part 7

Maggie welcomed the warm sunshine on her face as she waited for Eva to lock up the gallery for lunch.

"The pub does good home-made food but it will be busy with tourists, the bistro on the harbour is less well known but the food is great," Eva said.

Maggie smiled. "The bistro it is then, I'm famished."

"Great, follow me. It's a nice stroll down, too," Eva said, leading the way.

Maggie especially enjoyed the guided tour of the village that Eva relished offering en route to the Harbour Bistro.

Ballacombe's small centre was comprised of the ancient church, a village pub, a small post office which also served as a florist, a grocery store and a bakery which also housed a quaint tearoom and small bookshop.

The harbour was the crown of the village. Today it was filled with colourful fishing boats bobbing gently on the light swell of the current, and many small eateries clung to the water's edge. The bistro took pride of place with a fine sea view.

They found an outside table suitably positioned to catch the midday sunshine, and sat enjoying their chilled wine until they gratefully took delivery of their chosen dishes. Time passed comfortably, the two feeling as if they had known each other for years, such was the instant compatibility between them.

"So, Eva, do you live locally?" Maggie asked.

"Yes, I recently moved into my boyfriend's flat, about a mile from here. It's a real cosy love nest," Eva said, adding the latter as if savouring an intimate thought.

Maggie smiled at her "Love birds, eh? Who's the lucky guy?"

Eva relished the chance to talk of her beau. "His name is Pete Enders. He helps run his dad's building firm in Newton, we met there when I was working as a temp receptionist. You would have passed through Newton en route here"

Maggie remembered the quaint little town - she had stopped there for fuel.

"So, what brings you here Maggie?" Eva asked, and with an added afterthought, "Have you found somewhere to live?"

Maggie answered simply, "Change of job, new start, I guess. I took a short three-month let on a small flat near the post office, a respite until I can find somewhere more suitable." Though in truth Maggie liked the flat - it was cosy and had a lovely sea view.

"Are you married, children?" Eva asked.

Maggie shook her head. "I'm single, no children."

"Well, I think you are going to blend in just fine here," Eva said with genuine warmth.

"Thank you so much for being kind and welcoming on my first day, I was a bit nervous." She gave Eva's small dainty hand a quick, affectionate squeeze.

Eva smiled. "Look, you will have to come around for a meal one evening, Pete is a really good cook."

Maggie was touched by the gesture and accepted gratefully.

Her day ended on a high and she was filled with a sense that fate had somehow guided her here to Ballacombe.

It felt to her that the first piece of her life jigsaw had slotted into place.

Part 8

Ryan and his mother stood in the hallway facing each other, two gunslingers waiting to draw, the calm before the inevitable storm.

For Ryan, an overwhelming feeling of fear and anxiety had replaced the happiness of earlier.

Mother stood, holding him in a hard, cold stare her thoughts impossible to read. But the growing maelstrom was primed with a fury - more sensed than seen.

Her accusing words were the first drops of the deluge, before the approaching storm.

"You are late," she hissed venomously.

His mouth suddenly dry, the first beads of sweat glistened on his brow. He was not late, but to contradict her would incur a wrath more deadly than a scorpion's sting.

He considered this, and concluded that he would suffer either way, so drawing from a surge of courage he replied quietly, "I am not late, Mother."

His counter stance had the effect of a slap from an unseen hand; she was consumed with a fearsome rage fuelled by the fact that he had dared to speak back to her.

She spat back with acid-laced words, "You are the spawn of your father - he was a no-good, cheating liar too."

Ryan had taken most things from her over the years, just to keep the peace, but this time it was as if an imaginary line had been crossed, his long-suppressed anger started to seep out in a steady stream of molten lava.

Two worthy opponents primed, there would be no taking of prisoners in this last battle to the death.

He saw her eyes dart towards a wooden rolling pin silently waiting on the table, just within her reach if she was quick.

The knife glinted on the worktop. This was Ryan's preferred weapon of choice - quicker, cleaner.

Without further delay he grabbed it and in a sudden, swift movement raised it high and thrust down into her chest. Over and over again he repeated the thrusts, his anger was relentless, the room filled with the shrill sound of her death cries, loud at first, but then gradually diminishing.

Time seemed to slow as he watched her fall to the floor.

Silence ensued.

He had slain the dragon, conquered the monster.

Her death would breathe life into his.

Part 9

Maggie's first week passed smoothly. She had settled easily into her new work and her evenings had been spent making her little flat, homely and comfortable.

She had learned that she had replaced Barbara, who had worked there for ten years and was well respected. She and her husband Bill had decided to retire and move to New Zealand to be near their daughter and her young family, but it had been a sudden, spur of the moment decision, prompting Maggie's swift engagement.

In familiarising herself with her new role, Maggie had noticed how thorough and methodical Barbara's work had been. She was keen to continue in this vein, wanting to prove herself a worthy replacement.

She and Eva had enjoyed each other's company during the week and they were fast becoming firm friends. She had accepted an invite to go for a meal at Eva and Pete's flat that evening after work.

Her young friend's face would light up when she spoke of Pete and she would become dreamy-eyed when her thoughts were of him. She concluded Eva was most certainly in love and she found herself looking forward to meeting this 'knight in shining armour' who had so captured her friend's heart.

They were just preparing to close when Maggie's attention was drawn to the sound of the door opening.

She saw him for the first time, a tall, dark-haired man who now stood in the doorway. The effect he had on her was almost electric, making her catch her breath. He was aged about forty and ruggedly handsome with piercing blue eyes.

She hoped he hadn't noticed her stare as she spoke. "Oh I'm sorry, sir, we are just closing. We open again at 9am tomorrow morning."

He stood silent for a moment, but she noted he directed a brief nod at Eva before averting his gaze back towards her. She thought she caught his eyes take a quick up-and-down glance at her, but his expression remained cool and not particularly friendly.

He asked simply, "And you are?" His voice was deep, sexy.

She inexplicably felt rather shy and awkward as she answered, "I'm Maggie Watts, sir, can I help you?"

Eva coughed to catch her attention "This is Luke Drake, Maggie."

Her face started to get hot and she hoped she wasn't blushing but suspected she was. "Oh I'm sorry, Mr Drake, we haven't yet been introduced so I didn't realise, please accept my apologies."

His gaze was unwavering, penetrating.

"Well, we have been introduced now, Miss Watts. So, you are Barbara's replacement. She'll be a hard act to follow, I'm sorry to have lost her."

The obvious underlying meaning behind his words upset her a little, but despite this she managed a polite reply. "You won't be disappointed, Mr Drake, I can assure you I am suitably qualified for the position."

Eva stood silently, uncomfortable. She knew he could be difficult and this was turning into such an occasion. She was used to his brusque manner but she realised that this was Maggie's first experience of Luke Drake at his worst.

His response was nonchalant. “We shall see. I trust Eva has settled you in. Now if you’ll excuse me, I have work to do.”

He dismissed them both without further comment, entered his office and closed the door behind him.

Maggie pretended to shrug it off but the encounter had unsettled her greatly. Eva sensed her discomfort.

“Don’t worry, Mags, if it’s any consolation he treats everyone like that,” Eva said sympathetically.

Her inner voice whispered to her.

But I’m not everyone, and he is like no man I have met before.

Part 10

The day after he had killed his mother, Ryan was overwhelmed with a sea of emotions that he had kept suppressed for years. He'd kept them locked away in a deep, dark part of his mind, where they couldn't hurt him.

The desperate feelings of isolation, low esteem, criticism and constant fear, the longing for affection and recognition. They needed to be expressed, released.

There was another emotion creeping in too - panic. How was he to manage these feelings?

He held his breath, and slowly regained his composure. This technique had always served to calm him when he'd locked himself in the safety of the dark cupboard. The cupboard had served him well over the years during his many hours of need.

He came to the conclusion that he had a lifetime to learn how to deal with these emotions, but his first priority was to dispose of the monster lying in the kitchen and cover his tracks in some way. This was a time for thinking, not panic and despair.

One step at a time, he whispered to himself, one step at a time.

Slowly making his way back to the chamber of horrors he was relieved to see Mother's body still there. A small part of him had feared that she hadn't really died and would be waiting to berate him.

She lay in a pool of now semi-congealed blood; he sighed with relief that she really was dead.

Now, he must consider his options; his mind whirled this way and that with a sea of possibilities.

If he called the police and pretended it was a burglary he might slip up, give the game away, and end up in trouble. If he told the truth and said it was in self-defence he might be put into the care of social services.

One thing Ryan was certain of was that he hadn't secured his freedom just to lose it again. The horror of that thought kept his mind active and slowly he started to formulate a plan.

He would dispose of her body somehow and live quietly for a few days, just going to school as normal. He would wait until Betty came to clean on Tuesday; she was sure to ask where Mother was and he would tell her that she had packed a suitcase and left without giving any indication of where she was going, or when she would return.

He knew that Betty was aware of Mother's irrational moods so she would surely accept his story without question. Her disappearance would be attributed to her being unstable, a troubled character.

They would look for her of course - he wanted them to, to make sure they followed a trail of clues leading to a dead end. He knew this with certainty because he was the one that would create the trail.

Betty and Fred would care for him, he was sure of that.

He smiled to himself, pleased at his logical approach to this matter of inconvenience.

Now to work. Pulling out a chair, he sat pondering how to firstly dispose of the body. What would a man do in such circumstances? Well, he had no idea, but his mind veered towards Fred - what would Fred do in a stressful situation?

He remembered a time once, when Smithy had run off after a rabbit and got lost. Fred and Betty searched unsuccessfully for him and had been out of their minds with worry. He recalled how relieved they had been when the dog was found by a neighbour and brought home covered in mud and soaking wet. A sorry-looking Smithy indeed, ears down and tail limp.

Fred had had a few whiskies that evening, and Betty also, but only after she had bathed and dried the grateful dog, and put him to rest on his bed next to the warming fire. Actions so typical of Betty's caring nature.

OK, so whisky was needed. Mother used to drink from her secret supply hidden at the back of a kitchen cupboard, except it wasn't really a secret because Ryan knew it was there.

He helped himself to the stash now, not bothering to re-conceal the bottle afterwards - it wasn't necessary anymore because he was alone with only himself to answer to.

He poured a generous measure into a tumbler and swallowed a large mouthful. The instant burning sensation at the back of his throat made him cough and splutter, yet he persevered bravely. His head soon became light and giddy, but with this came a strange sense of calm - it helped him to think.

There was an exposed rocky hole at the top of the cliff that opened down into a small cavern, and it was only a mile away from the house. The geology teacher had said it was formed by the sea thousands of years ago at a time when the shore was closer inland. Now, however, the cavern below was dry and few people knew of its existence.

Ryan had read that in 1955 a local archaeologist had undertaken some rudimentary excavations of the cavern and had discovered bones of long-dead beasts, such as wolves. The poor creatures had fallen to their death and remained undiscovered for centuries. After the excavation was completed, the hole was covered over with a grid, but over the years it had become overgrown with vegetation and was barely visible these days.

This would make the perfect resting place for Mother, to lie amongst other vicious beasts. Though Ryan concluded the wild animals would not have been as vicious as Mother, not even close.

But how would he get the body there? He took another lengthy swig of amber nectar and waited patiently for that warm, calming feeling to overcome him once again. He considered that he could get to like this familiar buzz.

The car would serve as his instrument of transport. He was only sixteen and didn't yet have his provisional license, but he had watched Mother drive and confidently decided that he could manage the short trip to the cliff-top.

He thought about the protective grille covering the rocky opening. That hadn't been budged for years - it was sure to be bound by the roots of the resident foliage.

There was a crowbar in the garage he had seen it sat on a high dusty shelf. This could be used to lever open the grille covering.

Another long swig of the whisky triggered a spinning effect in his head, the ceiling appeared to close in and he felt a sudden wave of nausea engulf him.

He needed to lie down now.

His plan would have to wait until the morning.

Part 11

The evening was going well - Maggie had enjoyed the delicious meal that Pete had conjured up. He was likeable too, good natured and easy going. He clearly adored Eva as much as she did him, a couple clearly comfortable in each other's company.

She felt relaxed and at home with her perfect hosts.

After dinner they had moved into the comfort of the small lounge and the conversation had drifted to Luke Drake.

"He can be really difficult," Eva said referring to the recent unfortunate encounter Maggie had experienced.

Maggie nodded, the memory still raw in her mind. "The pictures in the gallery, you mentioned they were all his work. They have a slightly sad quality to them."

"And throw in a dose of secretiveness and you have his persona. Perhaps the pictures act as a sort of window to his soul," Eva said, then added, "but personally I don't care for them, or him particularly."

Maggie had to agree his work carried something unique and this enhanced her curiosity about the artist; she asked, "Is he married, children?"

Eva grinned "Gosh Mags, are you interested in him?"

Maggie blushed a little; she was interested but she hadn't realised it was so obvious.

Pete raised his hands in mock surrender "Oh-oh, if you

ladies are going to start talking men, I'm off to wash up and have me a beer," he said sauntering off to the sanctity of his kitchen.

Maggie laughed. "Nice guy you have there, and a really good cook too."

"He sure is," Eva said proudly "Kind of cute, too, don't you think?"

Maggie smiled and nodded in agreement; he was good-looking and nice with it, but her thoughts were of Luke. "I would like to know a bit more about Luke, I have to work with him and I would prefer to get along with him," she said.

Eva wasn't convinced. "Yeah right, Mags, but anyway, as far as I know, he's single, no children," she said, easing back into the comfort of the sofa. "Actually, I don't know much about him though - he plays his cards close to his chest."

Maggie decided not to push anymore this evening, but she was intrigued and wanted to know more about this mysterious man who she had only just met.

His spell had been cast over her and it secretly excited her.

Part 12

Luke sat in his studio gazing at the blank canvas facing him.

He was desperately trying to summon inspiration to start a portrait, which he had been commissioned to paint, but alas the juices just weren't flowing tonight. That happened sometimes when his thoughts drifted elsewhere.

At this moment his thoughts were drifting to Maggie - despite his initial reaction to her, he found her appealing, attractive.

Her work was proving faultless and her meticulous eye for detail easily measured up to Barbara's standards. He had noticed that people seemed to easily warm to her too.

He had listened to her talk to Eva and to customers and he likened her voice to the sound of a tuneful instrument, her smile made the room light up, her laugh was infectious.

He had noticed other things too. Her perfect curves that danced in time with her hips when she walked, she dressed nicely and always smelled alluring, she wore no wedding ring.

His creative juices were starting to flow, breathing life into the brush strokes, her image slowly came alive on the canvas before him.

He gazed at the beautiful woman that looked back at him from the canvas - he wanted her.

And he knew that he would do everything in his power to

win and keep her.

He always got what he wanted.

Part 13

Ryan's first date with whisky had left him with a headache, which he considered to be the worst he had ever experienced before, and that feeling of nausea still lingered but he really had to get on - he had work to do, important work that just wouldn't wait.

He recovered sufficiently to return to the kitchen and steeled himself for the task ahead. It occurred to him that he felt utterly detached from the scene before him, devoid of all feeling. But he had never felt close to his mother, so therefore it made perfect sense to him that you couldn't feel detached from something you had never been attached to in the first place. Arriving at this logical conclusion gave him peace of mind.

So with the blankets now positioned on the floor, he carefully rolled the cold, prone body onto them, rolling it up to form a tube-like appearance. After securing the bundle with string he was able to pull and half drag the body out to his awaiting motorised accomplice.

After a kangaroo start and a crunching of gears he had earlier managed to drive the car out of the garage and position it next to the front door. He had thoughtfully lined the boot with some plastic sheeting he had found in the garage - this would ensure the car fabric remained protected.

With a concerted effort he finally succeeded in his quest to get the body into the boot. He slammed it shut with an overriding sense of satisfaction.

He managed the short trip to the cliff top with relative ease; he found he was getting used to the feel of the car and felt more in control driving it. But despite this growing acquisition of driver confidence he still felt relieved to arrive at the destination without incident.

Parking close to the rocky opening he took a cursory look around to satisfy himself that his only companions were two nearby squawking gulls fighting over some carrion. Wasting no more time, he quickly got to work on the grisly task ahead.

His assumption had been correct; thick foliage had taken strong root around the grille, making it difficult to prise open, but the crow-bar succeeded in its task admirably. With some determined levering movements, the grille finally loosened and rattled free of its plant-like chains.

With much exertion he managed to haul the heavy weight out of the boot and drag it the short distance to the waiting rocky orifice. With one last Herculean thrust he levered up the body, feet facing down, and released his grip. Mother plummeted down to join her skeletal companions.

A sigh of relief replaced a prayer at the graveside.

No one would ever find her here, that is what he told himself as he threw the plastic sheeting and Mother's other belongings down into the rocky crypt to accompany her journey to the afterlife. The grille was replaced, thus sealing the makeshift tomb, and all fell silent on the cliff-top once again.

The kitchen was restored to its former self at the hands of some mop-and-bucket guests, hosted by Ryan.

Exhausted, the Game Master collapsed onto his bed, in the knowledge that part two would be staged tomorrow.

The work done, Ryan could sleep now, in safety.

As from a chrysalis, a different person would awake from this slumber.

Part 14

Fred returned to the warmth of the kitchen, hung his coat and sauntered over to the range to place the kettle on the waiting hob.

Betty heard his arrival and hurried to join him "Did you get Ryan home safely, love?" she asked.

"Aye, left him safely at the door." Fred sat down waiting for the kettle to boil, and suddenly felt tired after the day's events. He reached for his pipe and started to pack it with his favoured tobacco.

Betty could see he looked weary so she tasked herself with the tea-making whilst continuing to chat. "It's a sad lot that lad has been served. Not to speak ill of folk but she is not a fit mother to the boy and with no father either, I worry about his welfare."

Fred nodded, gratefully accepted a cup of tea and suggested they go through to the fire and the comfort of the lounge.

The lounge was warm and inviting, Smithy laid flat out on the hearth in a deep, contented sleep. This dog's life was to be envied.

Fred bent and gave him a loving pat, and thinking about his wife's words, he said sadly "Smithy here has a better life than the poor lad."

"I fear for him, Fred, sometimes - that mother of his has such a wicked temper, do you think I should speak to her about it, when I next visit?" Betty asked, bearing a worried expression.

Fred contemplated this silently for a moment before asking, "Do you think her aggression toward him is physical as well as verbal?"

"I've suspected it. I asked him once and he said no, but I've seen ugly bruises on his arms sometimes," she replied earnestly.

This thought troubled Fred "Look I think it's best if I accompany you on Tuesday when you call around there, we'll confront her together. It's just not right if she's mistreating the lad," he said decisively.

Betty drew her husband of thirty years close to her and hugged him tightly. "That's why I love you, Fred, there could be no better husband than you, and you are an even finer man."

Fred was touched by his wife's sincerity. "Well, they say behind every good man is a good woman, and mine's called Betty," he said, returning the hug.

They sat, embraced watching the flames flicker and dart, content that they had made the right decision to tackle this matter together.

Part 15

Eva and Pete had taken off to Cyprus for a last-minute late summer break, so when Maggie arrived at work that Monday morning she was fully expecting to be on her own.

To her surprise she found the door unlocked. Although the lock didn't appear to have been forced, she still entered tentatively just in case an intruder was lurking inside. But her fears were dispelled when she heard Luke on the phone in his office.

He sounded as if he had ended the call, so she popped her head around his door. "Good Morning, would you care for a coffee?" She asked.

He looked up briefly and replied quickly, "Coffee, black."

She nodded, but was a little annoyed by his lack of a 'good morning' or 'thank you' but despite this she still placed two chocolate biscuits on his saucer.

He made no attempt to get the door for her when she returned with the coffee, but she managed the feat with a graceful push of her hip.

"I have a lot of paperwork to catch up on," he said, and added, "as I'm sure you have."

Feeling as if she had been dismissed by the head teacher, she replied in a tone perhaps a little too cool "I trust it will be to your liking, but if it isn't I'm sure you'll tell me." She was glad to make her exit and assumed there would be little or no further conversation that day.

Luke busied himself with his work for much of the morning, and didn't venture out of his office. But he was unconsciously aware of her presence and had to concentrate on not letting his thoughts wander - he had work deadlines to complete.

Maggie was pleased at the arrival of her lunch break and, grabbing her bag, she made her escape for an hour. She had thought about inviting Luke, but still feeling miffed by his cold manner, decided against it and left without even a 'good bye'.

He heard her leaving, and sneaked a glance of her sauntering off. His eyes settled on the sway of her hips.

His desire was growing in the knowledge that she would be his soon, all in good time.

Part 16

The person who had been Ryan rose early that Sunday morning. It was 30 September.

He had the ten o'clock bus to catch to the nearby town of Newton, which served the outlying villages with essential amenities.

First, he must eat, and a bacon sandwich was soon devoured. He savoured the saltiness and relished the hot tea washing it down afterwards. His last meal had been over a day ago - adrenalin had been fuelling him since then.

Mother's bedroom had been arranged to look as if she had packed quickly - her passport, bag and purse, jewellery, toiletries all gone. The packed suitcase that contained all these items actually sat in her rocky crypt, but only he knew that of course.

Arriving at Newton train station, he made his way to the cash machine situated in the foyer, and withdrew £250 using his mother's debit card, which he had retained for this purpose - luckily he knew the pin number. He planned to destroy the card when he returned home later.

At the ticket office he purchased a single ticket in his mother's name, to travel to the ferry port at AImswater. It would appear that she had not planned a return journey.

He knew that he couldn't be placed at the station today with any certainty because he had done his homework.

Newton was an old-fashioned, quaint station and he knew it had no surveillance equipment installed. Also, he wasn't local to Newton so he considered it was unlikely he would be noticed, recognised or remembered.

He assumed the forthcoming police investigation into Mother's disappearance would try to establish her last movements. He had worked out that the cash withdrawal would place her at the station today, her ticket purchase would lead the search to Almswater, where it would of course become cold, because she had not boarded a ferry, and there would be no further movement on her passport.

Alas, the police would arrive at a dead end. He smiled at the thought of this.

What on earth had become of her, people would ask, but with no surviving family other than him the search would quickly fade into the background and eventually die.

And it did exactly that.

Part 17

Maggie arrived back at the gallery feeling refreshed and in a calmer disposition - the fresh sea air had revived her good spirits.

She noted Luke's door ajar and could hear sounds from within his office. She hoped if they had further exchanges today they would be cordial.

She need not have worried because he next appeared when she was in the throes of packing up for the day. She looked up to see him leaning against the door frame, watching her.

She was pleased when she noticed his eyes taking another quick glimpse of her. She noticed a dark growth of stubble had formed, which added to his rugged good looks - she found him incredibly attractive.

She managed a smile. "I was just about to pack up, did you want something before I go?" she asked, as she became aware of a slight nervous tingle inside her.

He had noticed her admiring glances, he knew she was attracted to him - her eyes conveyed it - this pleased him.

"We seem to have got off on the wrong foot, Maggie," he said. His tone and expression were unusually seductive as he continued, "It would be better if we got along, you and I, do you agree?"

His eyes remained focused on her, watching her every reaction - it disarmed but also excited her.

"Yes, that would be better," she replied a little shakily. "Are you going to be in all week?" was her attempt at continuing the conversation.

"For the most part yes. I have a back log of paperwork to get done, deadlines - you know how it is - so I need to be here at the office," he said evenly; he was in control of the situation.

Those deep-blue eyes and that penetrating gaze were having a magnetising effect on her.

"Well, if there is anything I can do to help, just ask," she offered pleasantly, trying to conceal her inner amorous thoughts.

"I think we should start over, Maggie," he said.

"OK, should we go through the formal introductions again?" she replied with a smile.

That smile, he found it strangely intoxicating, especially mixed with the aroma of her light perfume.

He turned towards the door and paused. "We'll have lunch tomorrow, twelve o'clock." He exited without waiting for an answer.

She stood in disbelief at his almost arrogant confidence that she would accept his invite. Yet, she knew that wild horses wouldn't keep her away from this date.

Luke switched on the ignition and swung the car out toward home, pleased in the knowledge that he had her in his sights.

He'd seen it in her eyes.

Part 18

Tuesday had arrived, and Betty was due any minute. He hoped she would bring Smithy - he would be allowed into the house today. Things were going to be different now that Mother had gone, he would see to that.

A rapping on the front door alerted him to her arrival and he opened it without delay. He was surprised to see Fred was with Betty, but no Smithy today, he noted sadly.

Despite his surprise he greeted them warmly "Please come in," he said. "Would you both care for some tea?"

They both smiled and Betty spoke kindly to him "Not just now, Ryan love, we came to speak with your mother, is she here?" she asked.

He was curious, but tried to hide it as he answered, "No, she isn't here, is everything OK?"

He noticed Betty glance at Fred; he took his cue. "Nothing for you to worry about, Son, just wanted a quick word with her. Will she be back soon?" Fred asked.

He decided it was time to tell them, so, shaking his head, he answered, "Well I don't know, you see she has left and she didn't say when she would be returning."

Both Betty and Fred looked confused. He had their attention, so he continued, "Well after my birthday she seemed upset and on Sunday she packed a suitcase and said she was going away to be on her own for a while."

Fred queried, "Going away? Did she say where she was going?" he asked.

Ryan didn't answer, he just shook his head, very convincingly.

Betty was frowning, Fred was speechless.

She finally asked, "Do you mean you have been here alone since Sunday?" She tried to keep the alarm out of her voice.

He nodded "Yes, but it's OK I have managed, I'm used to looking after myself," he replied.

Fred interrupted. "Well, that's not right, you can't stay here alone like this."

"Well, I've nowhere else to go," he said.

Betty spoke. "Right, it's decided, you go and pack a few things together - you are coming home with Fred and I, at least until your mother gets back," she said firmly.

He hid his smile at the irony of that statement, knowing that Mother would never get back.

He replied, "OK Betty, perhaps it's for the best," he said almost shyly. Fred ruffled his hair affectionately.

He had put on an Oscar-winning performance, and won the day.

Part 19

"It was Tuesday morning. Maggie had risen early, showered, and had spent an inordinate length of time rifling through her wardrobe wondering what to wear for her lunch date with Luke.

Her bed was strewn with discarded skirts and tops and an array of footwear littered the floor. She wanted to look perfect for him - she wanted him to want her.

She finally settled on a classy outfit that hugged her figure perfectly. She turned this way and that in the mirror until she was finally satisfied that she looked her best and she gave a silent prayer of thanks that her slim legs still held a slight trace of a tan.

She arrived at the gallery and spotted Luke's car outside - he had arrived early again. She concentrated on giving her best swing as she walked over to the door, hoping he might be watching her arrival.

He was. He noted how good she looked as the sun caught her hair - it was loose, wavy and falling seductively about her bare shoulders - her outfit did her figure justice too.

But he noticed something different about her look today. It was stylish and classy as usual, but today there was a hint of sexy and he grinned in the knowledge that the added spice was for his benefit. He was going to enjoy today.

His door was closed when she entered the gallery so she

didn't disturb him. The morning passed by uneventfully with few customers and as 12pm drew near she heard him approach her office. He came inside and sat on the edge of her desk.

She noticed he wore a loose white shirt and faded jeans, which fitted where it mattered. She felt a fluttering at his close proximity.

"Hi," he said, and for the first time he smiled at her.

Maggie was in awe, his smile was amazing. His deep-blue eyes seemed to penetrate her.

"Ready?" he asked simply.

She nodded. "Good, come with me, then," he said, stretching out his hand and taking hold of hers.

"So, where are we going for lunch?" she asked, climbing into his car.

"You'll find out soon enough," he teased.

He turned on the ignition and they set off along the coast road. She was intrigued.

They shortly arrived at the cliff top. Maggie hadn't visited there before but she had seen it from the distant view at the harbour.

It was mid-August and very hot, so Luke had parked the car in the shade of a small, lush copse. Maggie noticed the incredible view out to sea.

"That is indeed a fine view, but where are we eating?" she asked curiously, looking about and seeing no buildings.

Luke made a sweeping gesture with his arm as he replied, "we're eating here, I have lunch in the car."

She followed him to the boot and gasped in delight when she spotted the picnic hamper and cool bag. She was also surprised but pleased by the romantic gesture.

"What a lovely surprise - this is great," she said happily. He gave her that amazing smile again that would later most certainly conquer any resolve she might have against an amorous move on his part.

Blanket positioned and food neatly laid out, they shared the cold prawn and avocado salad that Luke had prepared, followed by crusty bread, slices of Camembert and grapes. Maggie had to concede it was delicious, and told him so.

After they had finished eating, Luke noticed the easy manner

in which she kicked off her sandals and made herself comfortable on the blanket next to him. He handed her a glass of fizz and poured one for himself.

She sipped the cool wine gratefully.

They passed a pleasant hour chatting, largely about Maggie's life. He was full of questions and she happily divulged her past.

Eventually she decided to probe into his life "Well enough about me, tell me about you," she said, taking a long sip of the bubbling wine.

He looked at her thoughtfully before answering, "All in good time, Maggie," he said, moving closer towards her. He gently took the wine glass out of her hand and placed it down next to his.

Her heart started to beat a little faster as his fingers gently followed the contour of her neck, slipping down to her shoulder and drawing her into him. She didn't resist and responded enthusiastically to his touch and deep kiss.

Pushing her gently down, he slowly pulled up her dress and delicately removed her underwear, she felt his fingers gently tracing her inner thigh upwards, and the erotic intimacy that followed was electrifying. Aroused, she loosened his jeans, exposing his erection, and gasped with pleasure as he entered her. Moving in rhythm with each other, they climaxed quickly.

The gallery remained closed that afternoon.

Part 20

This will be your room, love," Betty said, smiling warmly. "Fred has brought your case and school things up, so get yourself unpacked and settled in, then come and join us downstairs for supper." She gave him a loving hug before disappearing along the landing.

He nodded, and looked at his things carefully placed on the bed.

He took pleasure in knowing it was his bed, with its brightly coloured quilt, in his room. He could smell the heavy scent of beeswax polish, the old wooden furniture having been lovingly cared for by Betty. He filled his lungs with the wonderful aroma.

He had been given the loft room, which had a balcony looking down over the harbour. It was a lovely view and a lovely room.

In that moment he felt something he wasn't accustomed to - happiness, he absorbed the wonderful feeling.

Ryan, the boy, had survived admirably but it was a young man that now stood drinking in these wonderful feelings so new to him.

At last he had a real family, in a real home; he had a life.

Part 21

Maggie lay in her bed that evening with thoughts of their lovemaking - such longing and passion she had never experienced before. She thought of his touch, the way it had made her tingle with pleasure and she felt desire rising within her once again.

She wanted to feel that passion again, she wanted him again.

Luke had showered and now stood at his French windows, looking out over the fields beyond. He took a long swig from the chilled bottle of beer he held, the ice-cold liquid cut through his throat, quenching his thirst.

His thoughts drifted to her, her moans of pleasure as she writhed beneath him, the scent of her, the feeling of being inside her. He wanted to experience that pleasure again.

He wanted her and he made a promise that he would have her again, and soon.

Part 22

The next few years of Ryan's life felt as if he inhabited someone else's body and mind. No longer did he have to live in fear of Mother's mood swings and violent outbursts. It felt as if a different world had opened up and embraced him.

His days were filled with pursuits he loved and he had developed a love of art that served to express his feelings, which he otherwise struggled to put into words. It was very cathartic and helped release long-suppressed emotions.

He had become a different person, living in a different world.

Betty and Fred had waited two weeks before contacting the police. They explained that they had hoped Ryan's mother would return but with no word from her they had decided to involve the police, should some harm have come to her.

The police attempted to locate her but there had been no further movement on her bank card or passport, so their lines of enquiry soon petered out, just as he had planned.

Betty had managed to trace his father and he received an invite to go and stay with him. He declined and his father never contacted him again.

One conversation stood out in his memory. Fred announced that he would like to speak to him about a sensitive matter that was dear to him and Betty.

"We think of you as our son now, and would like to become

your legal guardians. Would you be in agreement to taking our family name?" Fred had asked with a serious expression.

These words had such an overwhelming effect on him - he was overcome with such strong emotion and affection for these two people who stood by him. His voice was raw with emotion as he stuttered his reply, "It would be an honour."

Betty had thrown her hands in the air and rushed over to him, tears welling in her eyes. She embraced him tightly.

Fred shook his hand firmly, and said, "Then I proudly welcome you to the Drake family as my son."

It was a memorable and mightily fine day.

The following year he went off to university but he always carried a photo of Fred, Betty and Smithy in his wallet, so he could feel close to them.

He kept himself to himself at university, as he had done in school, but he excelled in his subjects, especially in art. When he returned home a few years later he had grown into an accomplished, tall and handsome young man.

He remembered the day of his home coming. He had surprised Betty by arriving unannounced, crept up behind her in the kitchen and hugged her fiercely.

She had jumped in fright. "Oh, you startled me!" she said, her eyes filling with delight at the surprise. "My, what a fine young man you've grown into!" she had exclaimed.

"Hi Betty, missed me?" he said, as he returned the hug. "Where's Fred?"

"Oh, he is out walking Smithy, poor old fella is getting a bit shaky on his legs these days," she replied.

"Fred or Smithy?" he asked.

She gave him a mock slap on the arm. "Well, both of them," she replied.

They had both laughed at the joke, and he would always remember the occasion fondly because that day he realised that this place was where his heart truly belonged now.

Part 23

Maggie arrived at work the following Monday morning looking forward to Eva's return; she had missed her.

She found her friend sitting behind her desk, tanned and beaming.

"My, oh my!" Maggie exclaimed. "Didn't get much sun then?"

The two friends hugged and laughed together. "I've had the best time," Eva said happily.

"Glad to hear it," Maggie replied. "I've missed you so much."

Eva wiggled the second finger of her left hand in front of Maggie and she instantly noticed the diamond ring; she gasped, "Oh Eva, it's beautiful - so Pete proposed and, let me guess, you said yes?" Maggie said.

"First night there," Eva remarked proudly, "and I said YES straight away."

"Well, congratulations!" Maggie said, delighted - Eva's happiness was infectious.

Eva continued excitedly, "Please promise me you will help me with all the arrangements and you will of course be my bridesmaid?" Eva's parents lived abroad and she had no immediate family close by.

Maggie took hold of her hands, squeezing them gently, "Of course I will - I wouldn't miss any of this for the world"

Luke arrived in the midst of all this chatter. "So what's the celebration?" he asked, though he wasn't particularly interested. He would have preferred to whisk Maggie into his office, lock the door and make love to her, there over his desk, but he managed to retain his composure.

"I'm getting married, to Pete, you met him once when he picked me up from work," Eva said, all smiles.

Luke couldn't remember meeting the groom-to-be but he responded politely, "Well congratulations, can you pop in Maggie?" he asked, gesturing her into his office.

She nodded.

"Make it snappy," he insisted as he escaped into his office. He had work to do now but he wanted to see Maggie to arrange a date for later.

In truth he had never taken to Eva, the customers liked her well enough and Maggie seemed to be on really good terms with her, but he just didn't feel comfortable with her. He felt curiously threatened by her, so he kept her at arm's length.

Eva was taken aback that he had at least been polite. "What's got into him?" she asked, genuinely surprised.

Maggie smiled. "Don't know, maybe he's in love," she replied.

Eva shook her head in disbelief. "I would be most surprised at that" she said truthfully

Maggie laughed but shrugged it off for now. "Well I had better go and see what he wants," she said, and headed over to his office, secretly excited at the thought of being near to him again.

She entered his office and closed the door behind her.

"Come over here," he said.

She obliged. Swivelling his chair round to face her, she gently unbuttoned his shirt and let her finger gently run down his chest.

"So, what did you want to see me about?" she asked seductively.

He took both her hands and pulled her into him, kissing her passionately. "Come round to my place later, seven-ish," he said in breathy moments between the kisses; he pushed a piece of paper into her hand that gave directions to his place.

She took it and nodded. Noticing he was aroused, she let her hand slip down to the zip of his jeans.

He caught her hand. "You want me too, don't you?" he said.

She did; her heart was beating fast as she replied, "Yes."

"Good, but later," he said, re-fastening his shirt. "I really do have a lot of work to do now."

She kissed him softly on the mouth. "Until later," she whispered as she departed.

Part 24

He would never forget that grey and wet Sunday morning.

He had gone downstairs to breakfast to find Betty crying and Fred's eyes moist and heavy, filled with sorrow.

Smithy had died, peacefully in his sleep. He had lived to the grand age of seventeen and, although shaky on his legs, he had appeared otherwise fit up until the end. His passing was unexpected.

It was the worst day of his life. He had never lost something he truly loved, something so special. The emotional grief he felt overwhelmed him, and a strange feeling of numbness took hold and gripped him for days.

He couldn't quite accept that he would never see, touch or speak to his loyal friend again.

After a week he felt strong enough to be able talk about the loss of Smithy.

One evening when he and Fred were recalling memories of their lost friend he asked him why the dog had been named Smithy.

Fred smiled fondly and gave his answer. "He was just a pup when I found him, not more than four months old. I was out fishing and I found him tied with rope to the harbour wall, cold and wet."

He gasped in horror. "You mean he was abandoned, just

left there?"

"Aye Son, there's some cruel folk in this world. Anyway, I couldn't just leave him there, so I brought him home for Betty to care for," Fred said, taking a puff on his pipe before continuing the tale. "Betty fell in love with him straight away and insisted he was staying, for good. Never argue with a woman over such things, Son." He grinned and winked.

"I'll bear that in mind," he said.

Fred continued, "Betty's maiden name is Smith and she was very close to her father, Luke," he explained. "Well, we decided to call him Luke out of respect for her father who had recently passed away, but curiously the pup wouldn't respond to it. So Betty called out 'Smithy' and he tilted his head, wagged his tail. So Smithy became Smithy."

He smiled, recalling Smithy's quirky character.

"Betty always wanted a son and we decided we would call him Luke after her father, but we weren't able to have children," Fred said with a sigh.

He felt saddened by this. "But you have a son now," he said suddenly.

"Aye, we do, and mighty proud of you we are too," Fred said truthfully.

He loved Fred as a father, and Betty as a mother. Suddenly he felt compelled to act upon his love for them, to somehow acknowledge the kindness they had bestowed upon him.

They had given him his one chance in life and he wanted to make a gesture to repay them.

He spoke candidly "Words don't come easily to me, Fred, so I have never told you both how proud I am to be your son - I would like to honour that privilege"

Fred was silent, he was listening. "I would like to take the name of Luke, so you and Betty can have the son you both wanted."

Fred was filled with a deep sense of respect for this young man who stood before him, this man who was his son in all but blood. He said simply "that would be a fine gesture, my son," but there was nothing simple about the depth of love he felt for his son at that moment.

So, from that day forward he became Luke Drake.

But Ryan still slept, albeit quietly for now.

Part 25

Luke finally left the gallery mid-afternoon, in the knowledge he would be seeing Maggie later that evening. He had gone straight home with the intention of painting, but he simply wasn't in the mood. He grabbed a cold beer and wandered out into the garden taking in the lovely warmth of the sun.

The house was secluded, set back from the coastal road along a long gravel drive. Complete privacy, just as Luke liked it.

He sat relaxing, thinking about life, his life since Mother. He rarely thought of her these days but now and again she would pop into his thoughts like a bad dream.

Seven years after her disappearance she was pronounced legally dead and he was the only surviving heir, so he inherited the family house and what remained of his mother's money.

Mother had inherited the property from an aged but well-to-do aunt, and the house had served as the marital home, but his father had had no financial rights to any of his mother's estate, even before they were divorced.

Before his mother was declared dead, his guardians had arranged to rent the property; they invested this income wisely, and now it sat inherited in his bank account.

He was young but financially secure and very comfortable. He used some of his wealth to completely refurbish the family house, making it into his own comfortable residence, where he could also work from.

Additionally, he had purchased the run-down old fish store in Ballacombe - this had been empty for years and badly in need of renovation. With Fred's help they converted it into the present-day gallery, where he displayed and sold his art.

Relaxing now in the privacy of his small empire, he grinned at his good fortune since the demise of his mother. Murder had certainly paid off in his case, but he didn't want to dwell any longer on memories of her - he thought of Maggie instead.

She would be here later, his prize catch. He decided he would show her his studio and unveil the portrait he had painted of her.

There was another small room at the back of his studio but that door was closed to everyone, including Maggie. No one had ever ventured in there except him.

That's the way it must always stay, his unseen secret place, the keeper of his past life.

Part 26

Maggie and Eva headed down to the Harbour Bistro for lunch, eager to discuss Eva's wedding plans.

Unusually they found it full with no empty tables, so Eva suggested they saunter over to the Pirate's Rest instead. She assured Maggie that the food there was always freshly prepared and tasted great.

Finding a sunny table in the beer garden they thumbed through the menu. Two glasses of fizz had been ordered en route to the table, and they arrived now nicely chilled and most welcome in the midday heat.

Clinking glasses, Maggie raised a toast to Eva's forthcoming wedding.

"So, what did you get up to whilst I was away?" Eva asked.

"Oh, this and that," Maggie replied.

Eva glanced at her watch. "Well, we've got forty-five minutes to discuss this and that," she laughed.

A woman holding a notepad and pencil approached their table smiling. "Ready to order, ladies?" she asked jovially.

Eva smiled at her "Hi Betty, yes, I think we are - I'll have a prawn sandwich, please."

"And what will you have, love? Betty asked, turning her smile to Maggie.

"I'll have the chicken salad, please," Maggie replied and returned the smile.

Betty noted the order. "You look well, Eva."

"Thanks Betty. Oh by the way, this is Maggie, Barbara's replacement at the gallery," Eva explained and, by return introduction, she said, "and Maggie, this is Betty, landlady of the Pirate's Rest."

Betty beamed. "Oh hello, Maggie love, pleased to meet you. How are you settling down at the gallery?" she asked.

Maggie smiled. "Pleased to meet you too, Betty. I'm settling down well at the gallery thank you - Eva has been looking after me."

Betty nodded. "That's good, love, and how is Mr Drake treating you?" Maggie noticed the wink at Eva but was unsure of the meaning behind it.

"Oh just fine," she replied.

"Well, that is good, otherwise I would have had to have words with him," Betty said in a mock-stern tone as she headed off with their order.

Maggie looked at Eva "They know each other, I assume?" she said, referring to Betty and Luke.

Eva laughed "That was Betty Drake, Luke's mum," she explained.

Maggie gasped in surprise. "Really? I had no idea. Luke has never mentioned it."

Not yet aware of the association between Maggie and Luke, it was Eva's turn to now look perplexed. "Mention it? Well he wouldn't, he hardly knows you, and besides he never talks about his family. I knew because she and Barbara were good friends," Eva explained.

"I sense you don't like him much?" Maggie said.

Eva was silent for a moment. "It is more I don't trust him particularly - he is so moody, so secretive, defensive, as if he is hiding something."

The conversation was interrupted by the arrival of food and

when it resumed it was on a lighter note and a different subject. She found Eva's comments had given her food for thought, but she decided not to tell her friend just yet about her and Luke's alliance.

That would be for another day; she needed to find out more about this mysterious yet captivating man who had become her lover.

He intrigued her more and more, and she was becoming consumed with a need to understand why.

Part 27

Maggie set off that evening to meet Luke. Following the directions he had given her, she found herself taking the coastal road out of the village, the same route they had taken to the cliff-top picnic.

Just before the cliff-top she took a left turn onto a long gravel drive leading her to an impressive house, not visible from the road. The house was tastefully renovated and very secluded.

That now familiar nervousness was creeping within her again at the thought of seeing him. He had an almost electrifying effect on her but she managed to maintain her composure as she approached the door and rang the bell.

Luke had been watching for her arrival and, ready to open the door, he welcomed her inside. As he bent to kiss her mouth, she wondered if he could hear her heart beating, it was racing so fast.

"Welcome to my castle," he said with a sweeping gesture ushering her inside.

"A most impressive castle," Maggie replied, looking around the hall in admiration.

He seemed to ignore the compliment. "Glad you found me OK," he said. She caught a trace of his smile and returned it.

The hall was large and bright with a flag-stone floor. A

central wooden staircase curved upwards to the first floor. Maggie noticed a large grandfather clock standing on show at the far-side wall, its rhythmic ticking loud and noticeable.

Luke caught her interest in it. "A family heir-loom," he explained.

She nodded. "It is an amazing house, Luke, I'd love to see it all," she said.

"Then you better come with me," he said taking her hand.

She allowed herself to be led on a guided tour around the house. It was truly impressive; she fell in love with the place immediately.

The tour ended in the ornate garden where a bottle of Chardonnay awaited them, chilling in an ice bucket. Luke filled two glasses and handed her one.

"So, do you like my place?" he asked, noticing how lovely she looked.

"Like it? I love it. It is amazing, how long have you lived here?" she asked.

Luke didn't want to get into that conversation - he didn't want to have to talk about living here as a child, and furthermore he didn't want Maggie to know about that part of his life.

He changed the subject. "Come with me, I want to show you something."

Taking her hand, he led her back to the hall and over to a hinged oak door.

"This leads down to the old cellar, it's my studio now, I'd like to show it to you," he explained.

She wanted to see this private world of his, so answered enthusiastically, "Yes please, I'd love to."

"Good, take my hand - the stairs are steep," he said, pleased at her level of interest.

The oak door opened onto stone steps leading down to the

cellar studio. Easels and pots of brushes stood haphazardly about, complete and incomplete images on canvas were propped against the walls - it felt like a very real working studio.

"Gosh," Maggie said, simply taking in the view around her. She noticed a picture covered in cloth sitting on an easel.

He followed the line of her vision. "This is what I wanted to show you," he said, walking across to the covered painting. He drew back the canvas to reveal the image he had painted of her.

She gasped in surprise at the picture before her, her image looking back at her. She felt a swell of emotion rise within her as she took in its magnificence - not vanity, just profoundly moved by the way he had truly captured her.

He moved close behind her and she fell back into his embrace. "Words escape me," she said truthfully.

As they stood embraced, looking upon the image, something unspoken yet special seemed to pass between them.

It seemed so natural, and fitting of the moment, as he started to slowly unzip the back of her light dress. He let it slip to the floor then turned her to face him, keeping his gaze on her naked form as he also undressed and slowly pushed her down onto the floor.

As they made love he felt so strong, so in control. He softly whispered to her, "Do you give yourself to me, Maggie?"

She felt his breath on her face, and the heat from his exertion in his words; as she climaxed, her answer, "Forever," escaped in a sigh.

In that moment Luke now knew he was the king of his castle.

Part 28

After calling time on what had been a very busy evening in the pub, Fred collapsed into the welcome arms of his recliner chair, cradling a tumbler of malt whisky.

"I'm getting too old for this, Betty," he said tiredly, looking over at his wife who had similarly collapsed onto the sofa opposite.

"You and me both," she replied sympathetically, "it was busy at lunch-time too."

Fred gave a nod of understanding. "We run a damn fine ship between us, love, but perhaps we should consider hiring some help," he suggested.

Betty nodded. She did all the cooking and waiting on tables whilst Fred ran the bar singlehandedly. During the busy summer months it was proving to be a tall order for such a small crew.

"Eva was in at lunch time, with the new girl Maggie, Barbara's replacement," Betty said, glancing at Fred's whisky and thinking a small one would be a good idea.

Fred noticed and dutifully rose to fix a whisky for her. "What is she like?" he asked.

Betty accepted the drink and gave him a grateful smile. "She seemed very nice and friendly, looked in her thirties, smart, very attractive, too."

Fred smiled. “You matchmaking wife,” he joked.

Betty let out a giggle - she couldn’t hide anything from her husband; he simply knew her too well. “About time he found a good woman to wed,” she said playfully.

Fred laughed openly “You just want an excuse to buy a new outfit,” he said.

Betty extended her leg in a playful kick and tutted in a pretend note of disapproval. “You men, no romance, good thing us women keep an eye on such things.”

Fred grinned and returned an affectionate light kick. “I’m sure you’ll keep the situation closely monitored,” he said, laughing.

Part 29

Eva and Pete were enjoying a comfortable evening in together.

Pete had produced a delicious meal and was now pottering in the kitchen, busily clearing up the dishes. Eva knew better than to get in his way - the kitchen was definitely Pete's territory and she was fine with that ground rule.

She was relaxing now on the sofa with a glass of wine, satisfied after her meal.

"Had lunch with Maggie today," she said, slightly raising her voice so Pete could hear, but he came through at that moment and joined her on the sofa, nursing a cold beer. "We ate at the Pirate's Rest," she added.

He nodded and slipped his arm around her affectionately, and she happily snuggled into him.

"We chatted briefly to Betty, Luke's mum," she said.

"Betty is a really nice lady. So did you enjoy your lunch?" he asked.

"Of course, Betty is almost as good a cook as you, honey" she teased.

"Almost, but not quite," he said, laughing.

Eva smiled then added, "Do you know what I think?"

"I have no idea," Pete replied, wondering where the conversation was leading, but clearly she had something that was playing on her mind.

"I think she is seeing someone," Eva said matter-of-factly

Pete feigned surprise. "Who Betty? I thought she was a happily married woman," he teased.

"Maggie, you fool," she said playfully swiping a cushion at her lover. He successfully fended off the attack with a quick movement of his arm

"OK, why do you only think she is seeing someone - surely she would tell you?" he asked.

Eva tried to explain. "Well, that is the odd thing. She is sort of dreamy, in-love sort of dreamy, but I think she's not telling me because I know him."

Pete pretended to choke on his beer. "Well, it's not me, honey"

Eva chuckled. "I think it is Luke Drake."

Pete hadn't expected that answer. "Really? Why?" he asked curiously.

"Well, call it sixth sense, but when I returned to work on Monday there was a sort of private something between them, their interactions with each other had changed – more friendly, a bit flirty," she explained.

Pete thought for a moment. "Well, if they have got together, are you not pleased for them? I mean, he is reasonably well off and a good-looking guy," he pointed out.

Eva thought about this. He was right, but there was something about Luke Drake, something unfathomable - she couldn't explain it, she just sensed it.

She attempted to put this into words. "It's difficult to explain, I don't know why, but I just don't trust him. I think it is mutual because he seems to keep me at arm's length."

Pete was aware that Eva had never really taken to Luke - she tolerated him for the sake of her job, but he had sometimes wondered why she disliked him. He had never pushed it; he had just figured she had her reasons.

"Well, they are both adults, they can do as they please," he said.

"I know, but I just worry that he might hurt her," she said, stressing her point.

"Hurt her?" Pete said questioningly. "You mean physically?"

Eva shook her head. "No, I meant emotionally, I don't know, Pete, perhaps I am being silly," she conceded.

He gave her a squeeze. "You care about Maggie, so it follows if you have suspicions about him that you are going to worry, but she is a big girl now, Eva, you will just have to let her get on with it," he said, but in a kindly manner.

She nodded; she knew he was right, but despite his logic, she just couldn't shake the feeling.

A bad feeling.

Part 30

Maggie and Luke lay on the floor, spent after their passionate lovemaking.

"Are all these your work?" she asked, admiring the various paintings scattered about the studio.

Luke nodded. "All of them, yes. Do you like my work?" he asked, eager for her approval.

She did; the work was unique, unusual, dark colours, strong firm lines. They spoke of confidence, yet there was also an almost troubled theme lurking beneath the brush strokes.

"The pictures speak," she replied simply.

He did indeed paint from a place deep within him; he felt moved that she had recognised this.

"Quite the art connoisseur," he said softly.

"The work has a rare quality," she added with a smile.

That lovely smile that he found so alluring, especially here in the fading light. "You are a rare diamond, Maggie." He spoke from the heart.

A gentle kiss on his lips served as her silent reply. She knew now in her heart that she was in love with him.

Part 31

The following day, Maggie arrived at work a little later than normal, having driven straight there from Luke's place. She greeted Eva warmly and gladly accepted the offer of tea. "Overslept?" Eva asked, but noticing she looked different this morning - tousled, dreamy.

Maggie nodded, not wanting to explain where she had been.

Eva was putting two and two together, however. "Seems Luke has overslept too, because he isn't here either," she said.

Maggie answered without thinking. "Oh, he won't be in until later, he has some work to do." She realised straight away that she had given the game away as she saw a brief, knowing look cross her friend's face.

"And how would you know that, Maggie?" she asked teasingly.

Maggie held her hands up. "OK, I fell into that one," she said, defeated.

"So, are you two seeing each other?" Eva asked directly.

Maggie could see no further point in denying it. "Yes, we are, for about two weeks now," she replied.

Eva sat back, a little shocked - even though she had had her suspicions, hearing it for definite jolted her. "How on earth did you melt the ice man?" she asked with genuine curiosity.

Grinning, Maggie replied coyly, "Well, that would be

telling."

Eva managed a small laugh, but didn't speak. Maggie sensed something unspoken on Eva's mind; it confused her.

In a more serious tone, Maggie asked, "Do you not approve?"

"It's not that," Eva replied, searching for the right words. "I just … don't like him, and I care about you."

Maggie was touched by her friend's sincerity but still confused by her reaction. "Has he hurt you in some way in the past, or is there something you know that I don't?" she asked gently.

Eva shook her head, "No, not at all, I just don't trust him - call it bad vibes. I can't explain it," she said, a little frustrated at not being able to explain clearly the reason for her feelings.

Maggie took her friend's small hand and squeezed it. "Thank you for your concern, I really mean that, but I'm sure I'll be just fine. He is a very private person, but I love him." She spoke sincerely.

Eva gave her a small hug in resignation. "I wish you happiness, Maggie, just promise me you will be careful."

"I promise," Maggie replied.

The conversation troubled Maggie.

Eva's unexplained apprehension continued to grow.

Part 32

Luke took a late-morning detour en- route to the office, the result of a spur of the moment decision to drop in on Betty. He hoped that there might be the added bonus of a bite to eat, given that hunger pangs had started to dance in his stomach.

As if in answer to his wish he found Betty busy at the stove cooking something that smelled amazing. He hadn't eaten since lunch the previous day and after his and Maggie's passionate evening he was definitely ready for food.

He hugged her. "Hi there, that smells good."

"Well, this is a nice surprise," she said happily, returning his hug. "Would you care for a spot of early lunch? Fred and I have to open up in an hour."

"Why do you think I came?" he said playfully.

"Sit yourself down, love, Fred will be through in a moment," she said smiling. Her smile always mirrored the pleasure she felt in seeing her son.

Fred arrived and joined Luke at the table "Hello Son, what brings you here at this time - couldn't be Betty's summer stew could it?" he said mischievously.

"Won't deny it, I'm half-starved," Luke replied.

Betty jumped at the opportunity to do a bit of investigating. "You need a woman to look after you, keep you well fed." she said slyly.

Luke and Fred exchanged a knowing grin.

"But I've got you, Betty," Luke said, playing along.

"Tush," she said, not convinced. "I saw Eva yesterday, she introduced me to that nice new young lady, Maggie, very attractive."

Luke knew she was digging. "Really, is that her name?" he teased.

Betty gave him one of her looks.

"Actually, she is the reason why I have called around to see you," he said.

He had their attention.

"She is? Why?" Betty asked.

"Well, I wondered if I might bring her around to meet you both, perhaps on Saturday?" Luke replied.

Betty was pleased "Well of course, love. Come for around seven-ish"

Fred decided to intervene. "How long have you two been seeing each other?" he asked, genuinely interested.

"Just a couple of weeks, but she is sort of special," Luke replied.

Betty looked perplexed. "Only sort of special?" she said, more as a question than statement.

"Well, I'll decide whether she is or not if she gets the seal of approval from you guys," he said, giving her a wink.

Betty's smile widened; she was delighted at the prospect of meeting Maggie properly and getting to know her better.

Luke added, "So can we eat now?" Betty playfully swished the tea towel she was holding at him.

Fred shook his head, amused by the banter, but realised that this was the first time Luke had ever brought a girl friend home to meet them - she must be very special, he thought.

Part 33

For the second time that day, Luke found himself acting on impulse.

After leaving Betty and Fred's he had planned to head into the gallery to do a couple of hours of office work, but instead he found himself parked up on the cliff-top, listening to the sound of the sea below gently lapping against the shore, enriched with the cries of the circling gulls.

The tranquillity and seclusion of the place encouraged his thoughts. He had to admit that life was indeed good at the moment, but there had been many twists and turns along the way.

He thought about these now, about the person who had emerged, successful, wealthy even, and loved. He had experienced an existence without love for the first sixteen years of his life, and the memories of that time occasionally flickered into his thoughts, like now.

He had a memory of a boy, Ryan, alone, living a life of terror, but only the boy knew the full horror of that time. Then a day had arrived, a special day, when the boy performed an act of courage and freed himself from the madness that existed around him.

He had no memories of the boy after that day - he simply disappeared and was replaced by a person who promised to keep the boy safe. This person dwelled silently within him, this person called Luke.

Luke was Ryan's protector, and he would perform this duty at all costs.

Part 34

Maggie sat on her small balcony enjoying the view of the late-evening sunset, rich and golden, almost magical.

Eva's words had been lingering in the recesses of her mind, the concerns she had voiced about Luke. A part of Eva's personality that Maggie especially liked was her ability to see the good in everyone, yet she saw no good in Luke - she wondered why.

Maggie saw something special in Luke; he had a hypnotic effect on her that made her bend to his will, and she did so willingly. Yet, she had to admit he also unnerved her a little.

She concentrated on the reason for that now.

It occurred to her that she had told him everything about her, yet she knew little about him. During their conversations he had never divulged any personal details. She had learned from others that he was unmarried, had no children and that Betty was his mother.

She had to concede that Eva was correct in her assertion that he was secretive. Yet Maggie found that aspect of him mysterious and exciting. She wondered if her attraction and love for him had perhaps blinded her a little.

A mild curiosity was building - she wanted to dig a bit deeper beneath the surface of Luke Drake.

She wondered whether she would like what she might discover.

Part 35

Saturday morning arrived. Luke's hand fumbled on the bedside table for his mobile; finally locating it, he called Maggie.

He heard the now familiar voice answer.

"Hi, you have any plans for today?" he asked, voice groggy with sleep.

"No, nothing planned, you have something in mind?" she replied with a hint of naughtiness in her voice.

"How about I pick you up at 6.45?"

"Ok, what do you have planned?" She was intrigued.

"Just be ready at 6.45." He rung off.

Maggie was ready at 6.45, dressed in a delicate black lace dress and pretty sandals. She hoped Luke would like what he saw.

He arrived, looking his usual rugged, sexy self, which made Maggie's heart quiver. She had a similar effect on him and they let each know their reciprocal attraction by sharing a long passionate kiss.

"We can walk. I'll leave the car here and stay the night." Luke had it all worked out and Maggie offered no objection.

For now, the concerns she felt earlier evaporated to be replaced by a feeling of excitement in anticipation of the evening ahead.

She soon realised their destination was the Pirate's Rest

but, unusually, it looked to be closed, Betty and Fred having taken a rare evening off to entertain them. Taking her hand, Luke led her to the picturesque stone cottage at the rear of the pub.

"Welcome to my parents' home, we're dining here with them tonight," Luke said simply. "I understand you have already met Betty."

She gasped, genuinely surprised, yet secretly pleased by the significance of the gesture.

The contrast of his referring to his parents, then to Betty by name rather than 'mum' didn't escape Maggie's notice, but she made no comment.

"Gosh, I feel a little overwhelmed," she gasped.

"You will be fine, they are both very easy-going," Luke said kindly

That statement proved to be true on both counts. The evening went well - Betty and Fred were the perfect hosts; the meal was excellent and they all enjoyed the rest of the evening relaxing over drinks.

Later, as Luke lay sleeping next to her, she relived the evening. She had noticed the many pictures that graced his parents' lounge. There were pictures of Betty and Fred, pictures of the family dog, Smithy, pictures of Luke, and some family shots of them all together.

Nice pictures, happy pictures.

But a thought now occurred to her - all the pictures of Luke were him as an adolescent, or older as a young man. She realised there were none of Luke as a child.

How odd, she thought, as she finally fell into a deep slumber.

Part 36

Eva and Pete had spent a busy Saturday in the town of Newton, finalising their wedding plans; they were tired and glad to have found a free table in the crowded Fox and Hare pub.

No sooner had they sat down when Pete's friend Gary arrived unexpectedly at their table.

"Hi, just spotted you both, mind if I join you? There isn't a free seat in the house."

"Sure, no problem," Pete replied. He knew Gary through work; they were good mates. Eva gave him a welcoming smile, she liked him.

"What brings you both to Newton?" he asked, placing his pint down on the table and taking the seat opposite them.

"Wedding stuff," Pete explained.

Gary nodded. "Hey, Eva, who is that peach that works at the gallery? I spotted her last week."

Eva laughed. "That peach is called Maggie. She's really nice."

"She sure is." He whistled. "She seeing anyone?"

"Well, you certainly don't waste time getting to the point Gary," Eva said, "but your luck is out, she is spoken for."

"Damn," he shook his head. "I was going to try my luck."

Pete grinned at his friend, shaking his head in amusement. Gary considered himself a bit of a Casanova, always had a chat-up line ready if the occasion required it.

"So who is the lucky guy?" Gary pressed.

Eva told him. "Luke Drake, our boss."

"You are kidding me!" Gary exclaimed

"Nope, it is the truth" Eva turned to Pete, recalling their recent conversation. "She finally admitted it to me." He nodded his understanding

Gary whistled again, this time in surprise.

"My brother Ken was in the same year as him in school, said he was a real loner, always kept himself to himself."

But Gary then recalled something else his brother had told him about Luke Drake "Strange thing is, Ken knew him by a different name back then - he was known as Ryan Murton."

Eva and Pete exchanged a frowning glance.

This was the incentive she needed to do some digging.

She couldn't have imagined the disastrous consequences that would follow.

Part 37

Luke had left early Sunday morning. The afternoon was overcast and a little chilly out, but the aroma of coffee now gave Maggie a warm and comforting feeling.

Despite this, she was troubled. She had woken with a sea of questions floating like waves through her mind, and they all lead back to Luke. She needed some answers and was glad to now be alone so she could think.

Her starting point was Betty and Fred; after all, they were his parents. They had been landlord and landlady of the Pirate's Rest for years and they were both from local families. Establishing these facts from the pub's website had been relatively easy. So where did Luke fit in? There was no mention of a son on the website, and there were no pictures of him as a youth in his parents' home.

Question was, where had he been raised as a child?

She found a website giving a history of property occupancies, keyed in Luke's address, and eagerly digested the potted history of the property that slowly started to populate the screen.

It had been originally owned by a Mrs Irene Black; following her death, a family resided there - Mrs Celia Murton, née Black, Mr Ralph Murton, and a dependant named Ryan Murton. Maggie assumed the family must have inherited the property from the maternal side of the family, given the wife's maiden name.

Scrolling down the list of occupants, she paused at the next listing - it had been leased to a Mr Taylor Jonas. But it was the name of the landlord that caught her interest, a Mr Fred Drake. The lease agreement ended some years later when Luke Drake took over ownership.

Maggie felt confusion rising as her attempt to find answers had simply raised more questions, she sat back perplexed.

There had been no sale of the property listed in the period between the Murtons' residency ending and the rental period beginning, so how had Fred acquired the property? Similarly, there was no sale listed between the rental period ending and Luke appearing as the owner.

How did all these facts fit together? So many questions.

A strange enigma was unfolding, and Maggie wanted answers.

Part 38

Sunday afternoon found Luke sitting at his easel - he had been there for some time.

Creativity was not a beast that could be summoned on command, and today it refused to surface.

He was obsessed with thoughts of Maggie. How desirable, how intelligent she was and how beautiful she was, inside and out.

The way it pleased her to please him. The way her eyes shone with love when she looked at him.

He loved her and he knew he must capture and keep her very soul, for he could never allow that look in her eyes to die.

She must be his, all his, forever.

Part 39

Eva, the soon-to-be bride, sat comfortably in the Pirate's Rest snug, awaiting her soon-to-be husband. They had agreed to meet up after work; he was twenty minutes late she noted, glancing at her watch - where on earth was he?

As if on cue, Pete texted to say he was running late but would join her later. She sighed in resignation, and grabbed a magazine which had been discarded on the table next to her. She noted it was last month's edition and well thumbed, but it would pass the time all the same.

Flicking through, she paused at a page that featured old photos of local places. One caught her attention, and peering more closely she recognised it as the main entrance of Newton's railway station.

The station was quaint, old-fashioned, styled on a steam age now long gone. It had always reminded Eva of the film 'Brief Encounter,' the scene where Trevor Howard leans out of the train carriage, gazing lovingly at Celia Johnson waving goodbye to him from the steam-filled platform.

She noticed that this photo had quite by chance captured a figure of a young man exiting the station but recognised there was something familiar about him. She looked more closely, and gasped when she realised it was Luke Drake, a young Luke Drake, as a teenager.

What an extraordinary coincidence, she thought, him being

caught on film and, by a sheer fluke, her spotting him.

Still looking at the photo she noticed something circular hanging from the station's pub, aptly called the Flag and Whistle. Straining her eyes, she saw it was a clock, an old-fashioned type that also featured a clockwork date device. She noted the date was 30 September.

Eva folded the magazine in two and slipped it into her handbag.

Little did Luke know that a chance photographer had captured part of his secret, but he would know soon.

Part 40

Maggie strolled around the harbour, enjoying the crisp sea air despite the slight chill in the breeze. Being Sunday, most of the eating places were closed, but she noted the bistro was still welcoming late-season tourists.

Hurried footsteps sounded behind her.

"Maggie love, I thought it was you." Betty's familiar voice.

Maggie gave her a friendly hug. "Hi Betty, I was just taking an afternoon stroll," she said pleased that Betty had stopped her.

"Good for the soul," Betty said, smiling. "I just had to pop to the grocers for some tomatoes - everyone seems to want a salad with their main courses today," she explained in reference to the pub's dining customers.

The weather had turned a little cooler and Maggie shivered in the afternoon chill; she noticed Betty's cheeks reddened from the cool sea breeze. "Would you have time for some tea, Betty? Might warm us both up a bit, "she suggested, hopefully.

"That would be lovely - only have fifteen minutes, mind you," she said, aware of her kitchen obligations waiting.

Maggie smiled. "We'll make it a quick one then. I'll treat you."

They found a comfortable window seat in the bistro, and relished the arrival of the steaming hot tea for two.

"Thank you for last night, it was a lovely evening, Betty.

You and Fred were so welcoming and the food was truly delicious."

"Oh, it was a pleasure, love, and really lovely to meet you. You make a lovely couple, too, and that makes me happy," Betty said genuinely.

Maggie gave her a warm smile. She had instantly warmed to Betty, so open, honest and kind.

"Luke is lucky to have such lovely parents," she said graciously.

"Thank you Maggie, he is like a true son to us, we love him dearly."

Maggie's slightly confused expression told Betty that she didn't know Luke wasn't their blood son.

"We're his legal guardians, love" Betty explained.

"I see – sorry, I didn't know, but I did notice that there were no photos in your home of Luke as a child, and that did make me wonder." Maggie started to relax a little, perhaps there were answers after all to these many questions she had been juggling.

"He lived with his mother in the family home till he was sixteen, but after his mother left he came to live with Fred and me. He took our name and that of my father when he became part of our family, We all agreed upon that" Betty explained.

"I see," Maggie said, hoping that Betty would continue to fill in some of the blanks, and she did.

"The house Luke now lives in was their family home - I used to clean for his mother and got to know him well, he was a good boy but had a difficult time at home. His father left when he was just a toddler," Betty said, sipping her tea.

"What happened to his mother?" Maggie asked, trying not to be intrusive but also desperate to know more.

"Well, that's the strange thing, no one really knows. She just upped and left, abandoned him. The police tried to find her but she just disappeared. We managed the house and such things until, for the sake of the estate, she was eventually declared dead. After which, Luke inherited, being the sole surviving heir."

Maggie was shocked. "That must have been terrible for Luke, losing his mother in such circumstances, never knowing her fate!" she exclaimed.

She noticed a faint frown flit over Betty's face "He didn't have a happy time with her - she was unstable. He fared better with us and he's done us proud."

Betty drained her tea cup, lightly squeezed Maggie's hand and stood to depart. "I'll have to be going, Love, I'm needed back at the kitchen."

"Of course, Betty, thank you for your company - it has been lovely to chat with you," Maggie said.

"And you, love. Bye now," she said, getting ready to leave.

The two hugged and promised to meet up again soon.

Maggie sat alone at the table for a while longer, mulling over everything she had just learned.

A picture was slowly piecing together, but now another question started to materialise in her mind.

Simply, why hadn't Luke told her?

Part 41

Eva had got the bug.

Finding the picture had opened a can of worms in her thoughts. She had seen Luke briefly in the office on Monday morning and she had casually mentioned it to him.

He had acted with indifference, saying he didn't remember the occasion.

Eva considered the reaction odd. If it had been her she would have wanted to see the picture, if only to see if it jolted a memory. He, however, hadn't seemed surprised or even remotely interested.

She wondered if perhaps there had been an event on that date which could have prompted his visit. Encouraged by this idea she quickly entered a Google search of the date and general location to see if anything popped up.

Something did, and it made her sit back in surprise for the second time in as many days.

The screen before her displayed a news article relating to a missing woman, a Mrs Celia Murton, resident of Ballacombe. Her last known whereabouts had been the railway station at Newton; after this she had apparently disappeared. She recalled Gary saying Luke's surname in school had been Murton.

The article gave a number to call to report any sightings to the detective working on the case, but it also helpfully displayed a picture of Celia Murton standing next to her son, Ryan. The same teenager featured in the picture of Newton railway station, the final proof that Ryan and Luke were the same person.

So the date and location that Ryan, aka Luke, had purportedly forgotten about was the very date and location that his mother was last seen. Eva didn't buy it - things weren't adding up.

When Maggie arrived a little later, Eva decided to keep all that she had discovered to herself for now. She would find the right time to broach it with her friend.

Though Eva couldn't have known, that time would never come.

Part 42

Autumn had arrived, bringing with it a fierce storm - the back-lash of Hurricane Diana, currently wreaking havoc far out in the Atlantic.

The wind roared, whipping up the frenzied waves and the torrential rain was relentless. Diana would rage war over Ballacombe for the next forty-eight hours.

But a storm of a different nature was also brewing, a storm far more destructive and evil, a storm that would change lives forever.

This storm was inside Luke.

Part 43

The conversation with Eva had unnerved him greatly. He had kept his feelings hidden but in truth they were playing Russian roulette in the recesses of his mind.

He watched the storm outside, mighty and furious, a reflection of his own dark mood silently growing in intensity.

The chances of a random picture placing him at the station on that very day were so slim, but to be further compounded by Eva actually finding it. Fate had indeed caught up with him and dealt him a cruel blow.

He was nursing his third whisky of the day. It calmed him and helped him to think, and he needed to think of how to deal with this.

Slowly, the tendrils of a plan started to take root in his mind.

Part 44

Eva picked up the call on the second ring, she was still at the gallery.

"I've caught you, good. Do you still have the picture you spoke about?" It was Luke.

"I was just about to leave, but yes I do still have the photo" she replied.

"I would like to see it, in fact I would like to sketch it. Could you bring it over?" he asked.

Eva glanced out of the window at the maelstrom raging outside.

"What, now?" she queried

"Yes, I won't be in the gallery for a few days but I would like to make a start on sketching it," he reiterated.

She succumbed to his request, more to satisfy her own curiosity as to why he suddenly wanted the picture so desperately "Well, OK, I'll drive over. Will be with you in about twenty minutes,"

she said.

"Fine." Luke smiled to himself.

The ferocious wind blew her car about slightly, and she found her wipers were struggling to clear the deluge of rain driving against her windscreen. Her concentration was largely on the road ahead but she also felt intrigued by this sudden impromptu visit.

This was an opportunity to check out his responses first-hand, and she wasn't going to pass it up.

The wind moaned loudly, but he just caught the sound of her tyres crunching to a halt on the gravel drive outside.

She made a dash for the already open front door and was glad of the shelter of the hall.

Luke greeted her in his usual detached manner "You made it then - the storm is terrific, isn't it?"

Eva shook the rain from her coat. "Terrific, yeah. Um, is there somewhere I can hang this?" she asked, holding the dripping wet garment away from her.

He relieved her of the coat, and she found the warmth of the house welcoming despite there being no offer of hot coffee or tea. Reaching into her bag, she withdrew the magazine; his eyes registered the movement.

"Come with me down to my studio, and bring that with you," he said gesturing at the magazine.

She followed him down the stairs to the dimly lit basement studio. She looked around taking it all in - she had never seen an artist's studio before.

"Welcome to my studio" he said unconvincingly "the picture, may I see it?"

She handed the magazine to him, open at the relevant page. She noted how carefully he studied it, yet there was no hint of emotion in his face.

"Do you remember the day?" she asked directly, sounding braver than she felt.

He looked up, meeting her eyes. He didn't speak, yet his penetrating gaze was almost formidable and seemed to permeate the studio.

Outside of the gallery Eva had never been alone with Luke before, and it surprised her that being so now was making her a little nervous.

She repeated her question.

"Well it does seem to be me in the picture, but I don't remember the day, I've already told you that." His voice was hard, tinged with impatience or annoyance- she couldn't decide which.

Yet she felt compelled to get directly to the point.

"Strange that you don't remember…" she paused "…such a significant day."

Although he was standing in the shadows, she noticed a frown flit across his face. She was enjoying having the upper hand.

"Significant - in what way?" His manner was cooling even more, in step with his mood. What did this woman know? He was beginning to feel anger towards her.

"It was the day your mother vanished, Luke - or should I call you Ryan?" She made no attempt to conceal the slight cockiness in her question.

Luke felt as if he had been hit by a truck; his chest felt suddenly constricted, but he maintained a calm composure as he spoke.

"My, my, what a clever girl. So, what is it that you think you know about me, Eva?" he asked, his voice tinged with sarcasm.

The question knocked her off balance slightly, she didn't know, that was the problem, she had unearthed facts but it wasn't clear how they all fitted together.

"Cat got your tongue, Eva?" His turn to be cocky. He moved closer towards her, so close she became aware of the faint aroma of whisky on his breath.

"I don't know what I know," she stuttered, taking a small step backwards, but he caught her arm and held her still.

It startled her and he noticed it. His anger was rising like a mist swirling in his mind.

"And have you told anyone else about this thing you know but don't know?" he asked her angrily

She shook her head "No." She was becoming anxious, frightened by his darkening mood and manner.

So no one else knew about the photo - Luke felt a swathe of relief spread through him, but he also knew with certainty that Eva couldn't be allowed to leave. She may have been telling the truth about not knowing all the facts, but she already knew too much.

Her arm trembled slightly under his continuing grip - he felt it - it gave him a primal pleasure to be in control over her. He decided to teach her a lesson about who was in charge.

He pulled her into him roughly, so close he could feel her breath on his face. Noticing how soft her mouth looked he suddenly kissed her hard. She struggled, but then to his surprise she seemed to give in and began to return his kiss.

Eva was scared, yet she was inexplicably aroused - there was something magnetic about him which she couldn't fight, didn't want to fight.

Luke's building anger wanted to hurt her, but curiously he also wanted her. He pushed her against the wall forcefully and pulled her skirt up roughly, placing his knee between her legs forcing them apart. He kept her pinned like that against the wall as he loosened his jeans, lifted her up and brought her down onto him, penetrating her hard - she moaned in pleasure, he climaxed.

But within a moment she felt his hand tighten on her throat; he gripped and squeezed.

Their eyes fixated on each other - his cold and penetrating, hers desperate and scared.

He felt her last struggle, but it was in vain, she slowly became limp in his grasp and finally took her last breath. Her eyes once vibrant with life, misted over.

His grip loosened; he watched in fascination at the graceful manner in which her slight frame slipped down the wall and came to rest on the cold floor. The very same floor where he and Maggie had made love earlier.

He looked down at her still form, emotionless.

He wondered how she had found out, but the 'how' had been overshadowed by the 'what to do about it'. He wondered why he had treated her so roughly and cruelly in the end, yet strangely he had derived pleasure in doing so.

To satiate his anger perhaps, but he didn't much care about the answer.

She had crossed a boundary into his world uninvited - she had paid the ultimate price.

He did what he had to do, just like he did with Mother.

The bad seed that lived within him had served them both well - as he had once protected Ryan, Ryan had returned to now protect Luke.

Part 45

The storm raged.

Maggie lay awake in her bed, listening to the howling wind and the sound of the rain thrashing against her bedroom window. The apartment seemed to fearfully shake in the clutches of the malevolent force outside.

She was thinking of Luke.

She felt so sad that he had had to endure such an unhappy childhood in contrast to her own, which had been joy-filled, happy and content. This put it into perspective for her; she imagined how dreadful it must have felt to be abandoned by both parents, how desperately lonely and isolated that would make someone feel.

And yet Luke had somehow coped, risen above it, had become strong. She admired that resilience within him.

These feelings gave rise to questions - why had his mother abandoned him, where had she gone, to disappear so completely. Surely someone must have known where she was. None of this made sense.

It was 10pm. She wondered if he was sleeping or painting. He had told her that sometimes he could paint all night if his creativity was flowing. The work he created seemed to come from a place deep inside him, mirrored images of his soul.

A need was growing inside her; she wanted to hold him,

be close to him, tell him she loved him and promise she would never abandon him, as his mother had done.

She dressed, and battled through the storm to her car - she was going to surprise him.

She wanted him.

Part 46

Another whisky under his belt, Luke was thinking quick and hard.

He needed to get rid of her body, her car. He instinctively knew the storm was the key to achieving this.

He carried her light body upstairs with ease, replaced her coat and, after battling against the increasing force of the wind on his short trip to her car, he placed her body temporarily in the passenger side. He then rounded the car and climbed in behind the wheel.

Rivulets of rain trickled from his hair down to his face as he fumbled in her bag, finally locating the keys.

A sudden gust of wind caught the car as he drove through the blinding rain along the coast road to his destination, the Devil's Hairpin. It was a notorious sharp bend sided by a sheer cliff drop, infamous for accidents.

Applying the brakes on arrival to form skid tracks in the loose gravel surface, he came to a halt with this desired result.

He shifted her body into a sitting position behind the wheel, jamming her foot down on the clutch, and secured the seatbelt. Leaving the driver's door ajar, with gloved hand he carefully steered the car, allowing it to pick up speed as he approached the cliff edge. Before it lunged over the edge, he swiftly slipped the car into fourth gear, to all intents and purposes making it appear that she had taken the bend too fast, lost control of the car, and plunged to her death.

Should the police check the phone records of the gallery for that day they would see that his home number had called late afternoon. He would simply say that due to the terrible weather he had called to tell her to leave early. The question of why she would then walk the short distance to her home, get in her car and drive off along the coast road in such weather would have to remain a mystery.

Adrenalin racing through his veins, he jogged through the storm back to the house, arriving soaking wet. He said a silent prayer of thanks that he had passed no one en-route, but who would be out and about on such a wild night, other than him.

He headed straight into the shower, the hot gushing jet cut out the sound of Maggie's car crunching to a halt outside on the driveway.

Part 47

The house was lit up – good, he must still be up, Maggie thought as she steeled herself for the dash from the car to the shelter of the house.

Relieved to find the door unlocked, she hurried inside, the warmth of the hallway was instantly welcoming.

A shaft of light crept out of the door leading down to the cellar - it was ajar. Maggie made her way down, assuming that Luke was working late in his studio.

To her surprise she found the studio empty; a discarded magazine, open at a page of pictures, lay on the floor. She picked it up and placed it on a nearby stool next to a half-full bottle of whisky, but paid it no heed.

"Luke?" she called, but she was met by silence.

In the dimness she caught sight of another shaft of light casting an eerie shadow across the floor. It came from an internal door that was slightly ajar, she recalled it had been closed on her previous visits to the studio - she had no idea what lay behind it. Luke hadn't said and she hadn't asked but she was curious now, now that it was open.

She called his name again, no answer.

Gently pushing open the inner door she saw it lead into a smaller room, another studio dimly lit. As with the main studio pictures stood against the walls, but in the centre of the room stood an easel, a large painting rested upon it.

She moved closer to look at it. She saw a human form, female, the face painted into a twisted, tormented expression. But it was the landscape back ground that caught her eye.

It was familiar.

Part 48

Luke towel-dried his hair and pulled on some dry jeans and a tee shirt that were lying about on his bedroom floor.

He needed a whisky, and remembered he had left the bottle in his small studio.

Rain hammered against the bedroom window catching his attention. He took a moment to peer out into the fury of the night.

He saw the car straight away, Maggie's car. His heart skipped a beat - Why was she here? He wasn't expecting her. He felt a surge of panic but tinged with relief that, whatever the reason for her visit, if she had arrived a little earlier she would have witnessed the evening's events.

He rushed downstairs but stopped abruptly when he noticed the cellar door fully open. It hadn't been that way earlier; she must have gone down to the studio.

A surge of anxiety hit him as he suddenly realised in his haste to dispose of Eva he couldn't remember if he had closed the door into his inner studio, his private place.

If she had been tempted inside, it would change everything.

Part 49

Maggie stared at the canvas scene.

Behind the figure, there was a green copse with the sea in the distance. She recognised the scene but try as she might she couldn't place where from.

She looked closer still, straining to pick up any details that might jog her memory. She could make out something just behind the figure - letters, small and ornately painted into red swirls, making it hard to decipher.

Then it came to her, the green copse - she recognised the view - it was where she and Luke had had their picnic, but more significantly the spot where he had made love to her for the first time.

She wondered if he had painted the picture to mark that occasion, but she soon dispelled this idea as the woman was clearly not her and the date scrawled at the bottom corner of the painting was years old.

The red letters intrigued her - they appeared to have been painted on a small upright stone, yet she remembered seeing no such stone. She looked again, closer still. Slowly she started to make sense of the letters.

Suddenly she gasped in shock - she had deciphered the words and with it came the realisation of what the painting represented.

RIP, Mother

The stone was a headstone - his mother's headstone. Betty had said his mother had simply vanished, but now Maggie guessed her true fate.

At that moment she sensed him - rather than heard him behind her. She stood still, didn't turn around.

He had arrived at the door in time to witness her sudden reaction to the painting and understood what it meant - she had worked it out, she knew his secret. He felt as if a thunderbolt had fired straight through his heart, his head swam.

The moment seemed eternal, a hushed silence in anticipation of the final act of a play.

He spoke first.

"What are you doing here, Maggie?", His voice was flat, void of emotion.

She had almost forgotten her reason for coming, but slowly she remembered and replied, "I came here to surprise you."

"Well, you certainly did that," he said coldly.

He edged closer to her, his eyes tracing the outline of her delicate neck. He loved her, had had her in his grasp, she had been his, all his, and she must remain that way. He needed to remember seeing only love for him deep within her eyes.

But now that she knew his secret, that love light would surely die.

"what do you see in the picture, Maggie? "His voice softer now.

She felt apprehension rising within her, as she picked up the courage to speak

"I see your mother's grave Luke, it lies in the copse," she replied.

Now he knew what he must do - this would be hard for

him but it wouldn't stop him - he took another step closer towards reaching distance of her graceful neck, waiting there for him unaware of its impending fate.

She spoke again, suddenly, he stopped.

"I also came here tonight to tell you something," she said gently, almost a whisper.

She turned to face him, their eyes met as she spoke.

"I came here to tell you that I loved you."

The air was charged and his heart felt like it would burst. "And do you still love me Maggie, now that you know what you know?" He had to be sure - her eyes would tell him what lay in her heart.

She saw his eyes searching hers, for something, maybe for truth.

"I know that you were a child, Luke a hurt child, you did what you had to do to protect yourself. I still love you, Luke just as deeply," she said truthfully.

He believed her, the love still lived in her eyes he could see it. But he was also filled with a form of elation, because she understood, finally someone understood why he did what he did. He hadn't expected that, he had always believed that no one would understand why he had to let the monster inside him loose on that night all those years ago.

He asked slowly, "What are you going to do, now that you know?"

She thought about this before answering - she knew in her heart that she could neither betray his trust, nor lose him.

Finally, her answer rose from her heart. "It's a case of what we shall do now - we shall destroy this picture and forever put the nightmare behind us, we won't speak of this again"

He drew her into him and they held each other closely, words weren't necessary.

He knew now that whilst the flames of her love burned in

her heart she would honour him.

She would live to see another day.

Ryan still sleeps, and Maggie was his.

His secret was safe.

Epilogue

Rain trickled down the sides of the coffin as it lowered slowly into the ground, a reflection of the tears that now fell silently from Maggie's eyes, as she and Luke stood at the graveside with the other silent mourners.

Thunder and an overcast sky heavy with rain had added a fitting bleakness to Eva's funeral.

She thought of Pete - he had been so strong, but she had seen the depth of grief in his eyes, which mirrored his broken heart.

Her own pain at the loss of her dear friend in such a tragic way was beyond anything she had ever felt before. She missed her dearly, and still grieved deeply.

The police had been satisfied that on the night of the accident the poor visibility caused by the extreme weather, along with Eva misjudging her speed, had been the likely cause of her losing control of her car on the notorious bend.

Maggie thought about how supportive Luke had been, helping her through the loss of Eva, so understanding of her feelings, so sympathetic. She couldn't have got through this without him at her side. She slipped her hand in his now - it felt so safe there.

She would never know how close that hand had come to silencing her just as it had silenced Eva, to preserve a dark secret.

The demon in Luke sleeps, for now.

SUE EVANS